No Bad News

WRITTEN BY **Kenneth Cole**

PHOTOGRAPHS BY **John Ruebartsch**

Albert Whitman & Company

Morton Grove, Illinois

Library of Congress Cataloging-in-Publication Data

Cole, Kenneth.

No bad news / by Kenneth Cole; photographs by John Ruebartsch.

p. cm.

Summary: On his way to get a haircut, Marcus is dismayed by the bad things he sees
in his urban neighborhood, but after hearing his friends in the barbershop talk about
the many good things in their African-American community, he finds that on the way
home he sees nothing but good news.

ISBN 0-8075-4743-3 (hardcover)

[1. City and town life — Fiction. 2. Barbershops — Fiction.

3. Afro-Americans — Fiction.] I. Ruebartsch, John, ill. II. Title.

PZ7.C67349 No 2001

[Fic]—dc21

00-010521

Published in 2001 by Albert Whitman & Company,

6340 Oakton Street, Morton Grove, Illinois 60053-2723.

Published simultaneously in Canada by General Publishing,

Limited, Toronto. All rights reserved. No part of this book

may be reproduced or transmitted in any form or by any

means, electronic or mechanical, including photocopying,

recording, or by any information storage and retrieval

system, without permission in writing from the publisher.

Printed in China.

10 9 8 7 6 5 4 3 2 1

To Mrs. Wonnell and her
second grade class for listening, laughing,
and believing. — K.C.

Thanks to Claire for her steadfast enthusiasm on this project.
Thanks to Ron Zabler, printer extraordinaire. — J.R.

And with heartfelt thanks to the many friends
in our community whose kindness, support, and good news
helped make this book possible. — K.C. and J.R.

Every day, Marcus's first words were, "Good morning, Mom!" And today, like every day, his mother replied, "Well, good morning, son!" Marcus could already smell the great breakfast that his mom had fixed. It was his favorite: scrambled eggs, toast, and sausage.

"Hey, Mom," Marcus mumbled with his mouth full, "don't we go to Jackson's Barbershop today for my haircut?"

Getting a haircut was something that they had always done together. But today his mother said, "Honey, I have some things to do, so why don't you go without me?" Although Marcus had never gone by himself before, she knew he was old enough to go on his own.

All morning Marcus thought about the long walk to Jackson's Barbershop. "Are you sure you don't want to go?" he asked his mom.

She smiled at him and said, "You'll be fine." Then she gave him money for the haircut and a little extra for something special.

So this time he was going alone. A journey was about to begin.

Marcus knew the way to the barbershop. After all, he'd been there many times before. But without his mom by his side, he worried about walking through his neighborhood.

As he headed down an alley, he remembered hearing about some of the bad stuff that had happened there late one night. It seemed that all he ever heard about his neighborhood was bad news. "Is that all there is around here," he thought, "only bad news?"

Once familiar streets were now like a strange and faraway land. "I sure wish my mom was here," he thought.

The morning sun was warm and bright, but the neighborhood seemed cold and dark.

As Marcus got farther from his home, he began to see so much bad news!

By the liquor store, he saw people drinking from large bottles wrapped in brown paper bags. Although the men were laughing, to Marcus they looked sad. "Hey, li'l man!" one of them yelled. "Can I borrow some money?"

"No," Marcus replied softly. He walked faster. "Man," he thought, "people are even drinking bad news."

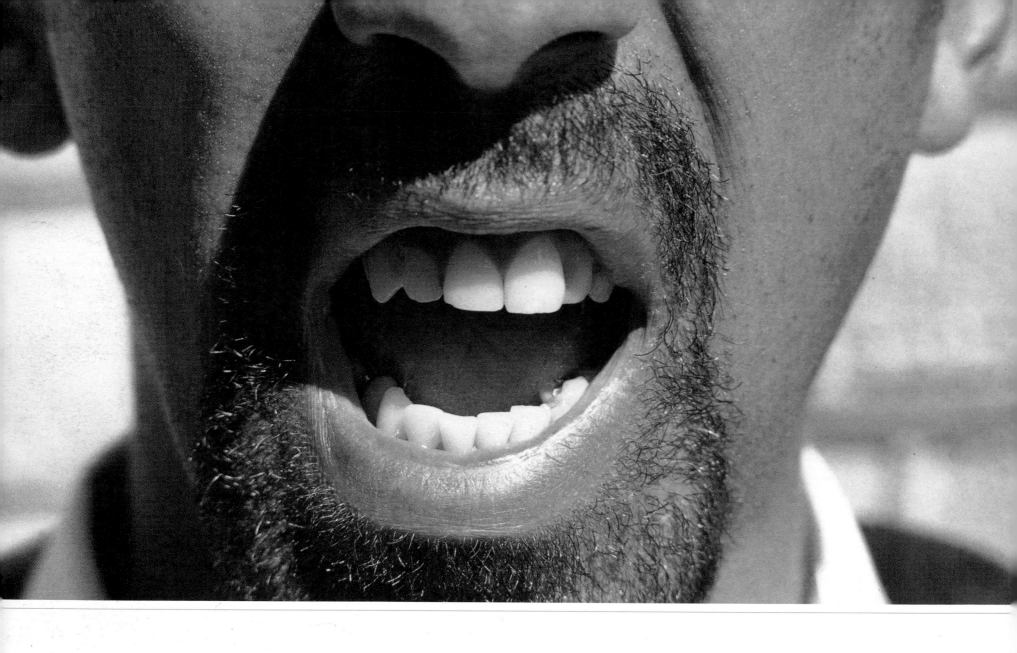

Noises filled the air, but Marcus could only hear horns honking, people hollering, and...

police sirens blaring.

All of a sudden, whomp! Marcus was knocked to the ground. "Watch where you're going, kid!" shouted an angry teenager running down the street.

Slowly, Marcus picked himself up. He almost felt like crying. He knew that things didn't have to be like this.

By the time he got to Jackson's Barbershop, Marcus looked as low as he felt.

Everyone in Marcus's neighborhood knew Mr. Jackson and went to his barbershop for their haircuts. Sometimes people would stop by just to talk or play checkers. "Well, well, look who's here!" Mr. Jackson bellowed as Marcus came in. "It's my favorite customer, and it looks like he needs a haircut!"

"Hey," Marcus said quietly.

"Get on up in this chair," said Mr. Jackson. Marcus noticed that today, Mr. Jackson was treating him a little bit differently. Today, he was treating him like one of the guys.

"What's up with the sad look on your face?" asked Mr. Jackson. He draped a large cloth over Marcus's small shoulders.

"Your head's so low I can't cut your hair," said Mr. Jackson. Then he placed his strong hand gently under Marcus's chin to lift and hold it steady. Click! Bzzzzzz! went the clippers.

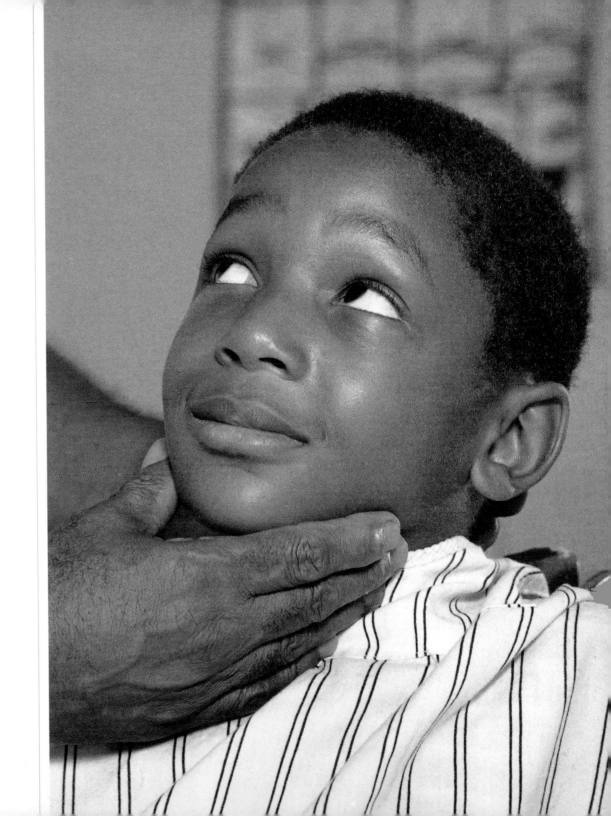

Mr. Kelley, who had been a truck driver before he retired, stopped his game of checkers. "Now, Marcus, I've never seen you so sad before. Why the long face?" he asked.

"It must be 'cause he's gonna miss all this hair!" joked Mr. Jackson.

"Nahh, I don't know," Marcus replied.

"Come on now, Marcus, you've never looked like this. What's going on?" asked Desmond, Mr. Jackson's assistant. Everyone in the barbershop listened closely as Marcus began to talk about the morning's journey.

Marcus sighed. "Well, on the way here I saw a bunch of bad news. I saw junky old buildings and trash all over the place. I saw people drinking, and some kid knocked me down!"

Clumps of hair fell to the ground. Mr. Jackson lifted Marcus's chin higher. He said, "You're right, son, there *is* some bad news out there. And it just doesn't seem right. Not right at all. But there's a lot of good news around here that you're not seeing."

"Really, like what?" Marcus asked respectfully.

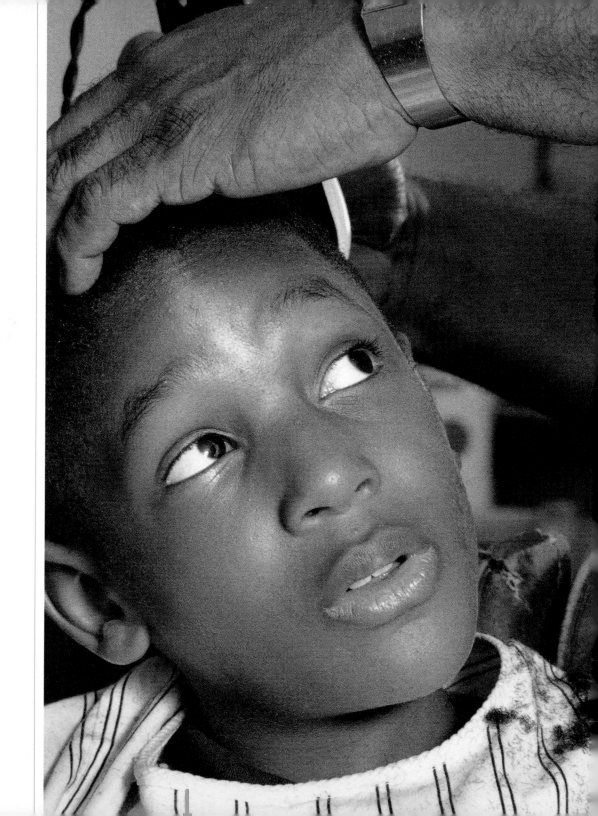

"Hey, what about the Wilsons?" answered T.K. "Both parents work hard jobs and they still take time to be together. Now that's some good news."

Ms. Powell added, "You probably walked past Ms. Isabelle's house. She's got one of the prettiest gardens in the neighborhood. You could say she grows good news."

Marcus listened as the folks in the barbershop reminded him and one another about the good news in their neighborhood.

Mr. Jackson said, "Just the other day I saw Mr. Alexander and his son repairing some old bikes. They fix them up and give them to kids in the neighborhood. You should see how happy the kids are to get those bikes!"

"Let's not forget my nephew Kyle!" Ms. Powell exclaimed. "That child loves to play his trumpet. Hearing his music just makes my day."

"And then there's Mr. Blake," added T.K. "He's been selling ice cream for over thirty years. When I was a kid all he had was a little cart; now he's got his own truck."

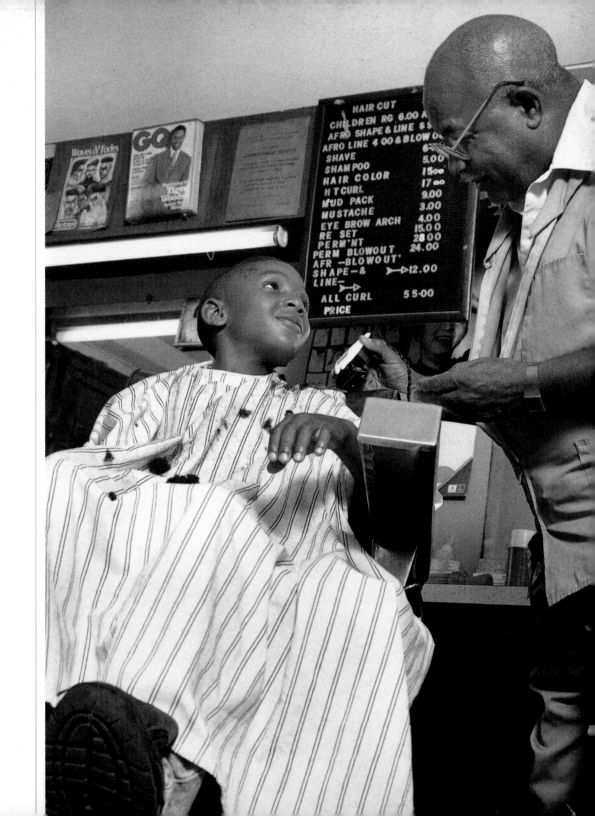

"Wow!" Marcus thought. What was to be a ten-minute haircut turned out to be an hour of history, laughter, and hope. Mr. Jackson spun the barber chair toward the mirror and said, "See how high your head is right now? Your chin is up, and you're proudly looking ahead."

"Yeah," said Marcus.

"Well, once you jump down off this chair, don't you let your head drop. Not one bit," instructed Mr. Jackson.

"Why not?" Marcus asked.

With the help of his cane, Mr. Kelley lifted himself from his chair and said, "Son, you can't see anything with your head held low. And you need to not only *see* the good news. You need to *be* the good news."

The haircut was finished. As is tradition, Mr Jackson handed the mirror to Marcus and asked, "Well, how's it look?" And to Marcus, things looked different.

With the warmth of the sun on his face, Marcus began his journey home.

He held his head high, and with each step he saw new sights and heard new sounds. Soon he met the Wilson family taking their morning stroll. "Good morning!" they said. Marcus had walked by the Wilsons many times before and never really noticed how happy they were together. But today, it was clear. He could see they were good news.

Before long he saw more good news. Mr. Alexander and his son were fixing a bike.
"Hey, Marcus, could you give us a hand?" asked Mr. Alexander.
"Sure thing!" Marcus replied.

Noises filled the air, but now all Marcus heard were birds singing, children playing, and people laughing.

Farther down the street, he heard little Kyle practicing his trumpet. The notes weren't perfect, but to Marcus they sounded just fine. "Good news sure is loud!" he thought, grinning.

And with the extra money his mother had given him, he bought himself a treat from the ice cream man, Mr. Blake. Good news never tasted so delicious.

He stopped for a while to see Ms. Isabelle and her beautiful garden. The flowers smelled wonderful. "Here's a little something for your mother," Ms. Isabelle said.

Marcus smiled as she placed good news right in the palm of his hand. "Thank you, ma'am," he said.

"Man!" Marcus thought. "The folks at the barbershop were right!"

On each block and around every corner, he found more and more good news. He knew there was still some bad news out there. But now, good news was all he saw.

As he came home, Marcus could hear his mother singing. He thought, "What a great morning!" With the journey complete, he rested on the steps thinking about all that he had learned and how much he had changed that day.

And as he looked around his neighborhood he realized, "There's even more good news out there. And I'm not just gonna find it…

I'm gonna make it!"